Mr. Lincoln's Way

To the 4th Grade Students of
Schoolcraft V.E.

Patricia Polacco. 2005

PATRICIA POLACCO

Mr. Lincoln's Way

PHILOMEL BOOKS

Mr. Lincoln was the coolest principal in the whole world, or so his students thought. He had the coolest clothes, had the coolest smile, and did the coolest things. He had tea parties with Mrs. West's kindergarten every spring. He took Mr. Bliss's sixth-graders on nature walks in the fall. He set up his telescope next to the pond in back of school on special nights and invited kids and their families to come and look at the stars.

And in the winter he was Santa for the Christmas play, lit the menorah for Chanukah, wore a dashiki for Kwanzaa and a burnoose for Ramadan.

Mr. Lincoln was just plain cool!

Absolutely everybody thought so except Eugene Esterhause. "Mean Gene" is what everybody called him. Mean Gene sassed the teachers and beat up on most of the other kids on the playground. He was no student at all. He drove Mrs. Dunkle crazy in English, Ms. Chu wanted to drop him from art.

And he was a bully. He always seemed angry, picking on kids and calling them names.

"He's not a bad boy, really," Mr. Lincoln said. "Only troubled."

To just about everybody in school, though, Eugene WAS trouble, spelled with a capital *T*.

Then one day he leered at a first-grader. "What you lookin' at, scumball?" he said, and he pushed her down and wrenched her backpack away.

"I'm going to tell Mr. Lincoln," she announced.

"Go ahead, you little brat. I ain't afraid of that n—" Then he stopped. Mr. Lincoln was standing right there.

The bell rang and Eugene scurried away.

Now Eugene was in Mr. Lincoln's thoughts more than ever— he knew he *had* to find a way to reach him.

Then one day as Mr. Lincoln was helping the fifth grade plant a tree in the beautiful new atrium, he noticed that Eugene was looking up into the branches of one of the other trees. There sat a bright red cardinal. Two other days Mr. Lincoln had seen Eugene standing at the atrium window, watching birds on the trees.

Mr. Lincoln wondered. Was it possible that . . .

It wasn't a day later when Mr. Lincoln called Eugene into his office. Eugene slumped into a chair. Mr. Lincoln took a beautiful book out of his desk drawer—a book in blazing color and all about birds! He turned to one page and studied the illustration. "I've got these little birds all over my tree, and I don't know what they are."

Eugene got out of his chair and walked closer. "Those are red-capped nuthatches. Weird to see them this time of year."

"You seem to know your birds!" Mr. Lincoln said with a warm smile.

"I do. When I lived on my grampa's farm, he had tons of birds around—chickens, thrashers, meadowlarks. We raised carrier pigeons together."

"You've got quite a grandpa," Mr. Lincoln said, but Eugene just turned his back on Mr. Lincoln and left the room.

A week had gone by when Eugene ran into Mr. Lincoln by the atrium, looking glum. "I have a problem," Mr. Lincoln said.

"So?"

"That atrium was supposed to be full of birds. But they're just not coming." The principal looked into the empty atrium.

"Wrong plants in there to make them want to stay. Not the right food, either." Eugene started to walk away.

"Your grandpa teach you that?"

Eugene turned and looked at Mr. Lincoln for the first time.

"Maybe."

"Do you suppose you could help us attract birds here to our atrium, Eugene?" Mr. Lincoln handed him a book. "And perhaps this would help."

Eugene seemed stunned at first. Then he took the beautiful book on birds in his hands, wrapped it in his arms, and bolted down the hall.

As the days passed, Eugene never seemed to be without the book. His English teacher let Eugene read passages from the book in class. "I'm so pleased to see him reading," Mrs. Dunkle exclaimed. And when he didn't have his nose in that book, he was almost constantly out in the atrium! He and Mr. Lincoln made a list of plants and shrubs to buy, and types of grain and seeds to feed the birds.

They even built three feeders together.

That's when it started to happen. The birds began to come!
Nuthatches, bluebirds, a tanager, and many colored finches. So
many different kinds that the whole school stood from time to time
just to watch the wonder of them in the atrium.

Eugene seemed genuinely happy. He didn't even tease other kids
anymore.

Then one day Miss Chu burst into Mr. Lincoln's office. "There are two mallards nesting in the atrium!"

Mr. Lincoln rushed to the hall, and sure enough there in the atrium were a male and female mallard. And there was their nest near the southeastern corner of the atrium. Mr. Lincoln saw Eugene on the other side of the atrium, giving him a thumbs-up.

"I was hoping that they might be a mating pair," Eugene said one day as he and Mr. Lincoln looked at the five perfect eggs in the nest. "Just one problem. The ducklings will need to be near water. They'll need to get to the pond outside. They can't fly out of the top like their parents."

"You'll think of something, Eugene. I know you will," Mr. Lincoln said. And he put his hand on Eugene's shoulder.

It was nice that "Mean Gene" wasn't mean anymore.

It was only three days later that there was a commotion in the hall. Mrs. Belding rushed into Mr. Lincoln's office with Eugene in tow.

Mr. Lincoln looked at Eugene in disbelief. "What happened?"

"I'll let Eugene tell you," Mrs. Belding trumpeted.

But Eugene said nothing. He just sat looking hateful and defiant.

"Trouble in the lunch line," she went on. "He singled out two of our students from Mexico—he called them brown-skinned toads, and other unacceptable names."

"I'll take care of this," Mr. Lincoln said quietly.

Mr. Lincoln sat down in front of the boy. "Eugene, my skin is brown, too."

Eugene just glared at Mr. Lincoln.

"This I know, Eugene—someone who loves birds the way you do couldn't possibly have that kind of hate in his heart."

Then Eugene began to cry. "My old man got real mad when I got home late from helping you." He sobbed. "He said you're not our kind."

"Our kind," Mr. Lincoln murmured. He led Eugene to the window of the atrium. It was alive with the songs of the birds. "I see sparrows, jays, cardinals, nuthatches . . . and the mallards. Don't all of those beautiful types and colors make this a beautiful place to be—for all of them?"

Eugene nodded yes.

"Well, God made all of them! All kinds! Just like he made all of us, Eugene. Fact is, all of you children here—with all of your cool differences—are my little birds. Yes, my little birds. And that should be your answer as to what is right or wrong in what your father said," Mr. Lincoln said quietly.

"My old man calls you real bad names, Mr. Lincoln. He's got an ugly name for just about everybody that's different from us."

Mr. Lincoln didn't talk for the longest time. "Eugene, sometimes people get trapped in their thinking almost as surely as those ducklings will be trapped in that atrium," Mr. Lincoln said thoughtfully.

"My grampa just wasn't like that."

Mr. Lincoln put his arm around the boy's shoulder. "I'd like to meet that grandpa. But Eugene, you have to promise me. Even when bad things happen at home, here at school you need to treat all of my little birds with kindness and respect. No more teasing and name-calling! Please promise me."

Eugene promised.

Eugene was good to his word. He became a model citizen. He tried with all of his heart to keep his promise to Mr. Lincoln. Then, one bright morning Eugene stopped at the atrium window. The eggs were starting to

hatch. He ran from room to room and brought the whole school to watch.

The ducklings were hatching one by one! At first they were wet and unsteady, but in a short time they were fuzzy and racing about.

As the days passed, the mallard parents flew out of the atrium, landing on the pond just behind the school. They were leaving their babies for longer and longer periods of time. Eugene and Mr. Lincoln knew that the time was approaching when they would need to get the ducklings out of the atrium and into the pond. They had a plan.

When the big day arrived, classes were asked to stay in their rooms.
Then Eugene and Mr. Lincoln opened the door to the atrium and
stepped in. They had both practiced saying "Ging . . . ging," like the
mallard parents. Now they talked to the ducklings, coaxing them to follow.

The father mallard waddled up to the doorway of the atrium and peered down the hall. At the end of the hall the father mallard could see the lawn and the pond.

"Ging . . . ging," Eugene called.

The mother mallard came out first, then one by one her babies followed. Eugene walked down the hall, calling to them over and over, as the family waddled behind him.

Then all at once the mother and father took the lead, and the ducklings scurried after them. At the outside doorway, they stopped for a moment, then the mother and father mallard jumped out of the doorway and coaxed each of the ducklings to follow.

Mr. Lincoln and Eugene both stood and watched as the ducklings raced down the hillside and plopped into the pond with their parents.

"Now I know where the expression 'like a duck takes to water' comes from." Mr. Lincoln laughed. He couldn't believe how well the babies swam.

Parents had gathered at the top of the hill—they had been invited to watch from afar. Then Eugene heard a voice from behind them call out his name. "Eugene! Boy, over here!"

It was his grandfather! The boy raced up the hill. Mr. Lincoln joined them both.

"This is my grampa!" Eugene sang out.

"I know," Mr. Lincoln said.

Eugene turned toward him. Had Mr. Lincoln something to do with this miracle, with his grampa being here?

Now the old man shook Mr. Lincoln's hand heartily.

"I would sure like to stay with you again, Grampa," Eugene said as he and his grandfather walked up the hill together.

The old man put his arm around the boy's shoulders. "We'll see, son. We'll sure see," he said.

Later Eugene and Mr. Lincoln walked down by the pond together.
Eugene needed to say something to Mr. Lincoln.

"You showed those ducklings the way out, Eugene," Mr. Lincoln said.

"Hey, you showed me the way out, Mr. Lincoln." Eugene smiled.
Then he stopped and looked into his principal's eyes.

"I'll make you proud of me, Mr. Lincoln. I promise."

Eugene Esterhause was true to his promise. He became a fourth-grade teacher . . . and called his students "my little birds."

PATRICIA LEE GAUCH, EDITOR

Text and illustrations copyright © 2001 by Babushka Inc. All rights reserved.
This book, or parts thereof, may not be reproduced in any form without permission in writing from the publisher,
PHILOMEL BOOKS
a division of Penguin Putnam Books for Young Readers,
345 Hudson Street, New York, NY 10014.
Philomel Books, Reg. U.S. Pat. & Tm. Off. Published simultaneously in Canada.
Manufactured in China by South China Printing Co. (1988) Ltd.
Book design by Semadar Megged.   The text is set in 14-point Goudy.

Library of Congress Cataloging-in-Publication Data
Polacco, Patricia.   Mr. Lincoln's way / Patricia Polacco.   p. cm.
Summary: When Mr. Lincoln, "the coolest principal in the whole world," discovers that Eugene,
the school bully, knows a lot about birds, he uses this interest to help Eugene overcome his intolerance.
[1. Prejudices—Fiction. 2. Birds—Fiction. 3. School principals—Fiction. 4. Bullies—Fiction.
5. Schools—Fiction.] I. Title. PZ7.P75186 Mn 2001 [Fic]—dc21   00-066939
ISBN 0-399-23754-2
7 9 10 8